Meet Mystabella and Rainbow Sparkles

SIZZLE PRESS

Meet Mystabella and Rainbow Sparkles

Are you ready to learn everything about this inseparable pair? Keep reading this guide and help our fantastic new friends solve puzzles as you go. But first, let's introduce the dazzling duo.

Mystabella and Rainbow Sparkles come from a magical land full of endless rainbows, cotton candy clouds, and everlasting friendships.

Sweet-tempered Mystabella is kind, caring, and trusting. She loves to help others and always sees the good in people.

Rainbow Sparkles has a heart of gold and would do anything for her best friend, Mystabella. She's extremely organized and isn't afraid to speak her mind.

Rainbow Rush

Rainbow Sparkles is in a rush to meet Mystabella at the rainbow, but which path gets her there first? The path with the least number of obstacles will be the fastest.

Sugary Shadows

Can you spot which shadow belongs to Rainbow Sparkles?

Fashion Friends: Dress Sense

Mystabella and Rainbow Sparkles always dress to impress. They love to experiment with style and can't resist soft pinks, blues, and yellows.

Mystabella loves to be a little adventurous with her outfits. As long as her clothes are covered in glitter and shiny rainbows, she's a happy shopper. She's always wearing wings, stars, and anything inspired by her love of unicorns!

Rainbow Sparkles is a big fan of stars, clouds, and, unsurprisingly, rainbows. She loves frills but has to be comfortable.

8

Dazzling Dress

Mystabella has been shopping. Color in and use your stickers to decorate the beautiful dress she bought.

Stylish Shopper

Rainbow Sparkles has bought a new party dress. Color in and use your stickers to decorate it.

Singing Stars: Jobs

Mystabella and Rainbow Sparkles make a great team!

Mystabella has always believed that a song can change the heart. She loves to sing, dance, and act, and when it comes to her dreams, the sky is the limit! Mystabella is on her way to becoming a superstar and she is lucky to have Rainbow Sparkles by her side to help her get there.

Rainbow Sparkles is the ultimate friend and manager. Timely, organized, and strong-minded, she believes there's nothing an organized checklist can't solve.

Together, these two are unstoppable!

Rainbow Race

Race up and down the rainbow to get to the star-studded stage for your grand pop performance.

How to play:

All players should begin at square one. Take turns rolling the die and making your way around the board. If you land at the bottom of a twirly rainbow, twirl your way up to the top. But if you land at the top of a straight rainbow, you must slide back down again! You must move the number of spaces that you roll. If you land on an instruction square, you must read it aloud and follow the instruction. The first player to reach the finish is the winner.

What you need:

- Coins to use as counters
- Counter stickers from your sticker sheet
- A die

29 Your head is in the clouds. You've forgotten your lyrics. Go back two spaces.

30

28

27

15

16 Your adoring fans stop you and ask for autographs. Miss a turn.

14

13

1 START

2

32 You're uniquely determined! Prance forward one space.

33

34

35 FINISH

25

24

23

22

18

19 There are stars in your eyes! You're so excited to arrive. Roll again.

20

21

11

10

9

8

4

5

6

7 Remember you have wings! Fly forward two spaces.

Planet Protectors:
Hobbies

The life of a busy singing sensation and her manager can be exhausting, but that doesn't stop these two from making the most of their spare time.

Mystabella's favorite hobby is aerial acrobatics. She loves to slide down rainbows and gracefully twirl through clouds. The higher she can get, the better!

Rainbow Sparkles is not quite so adventurous. She loves reading and listening to music, especially if it's her best friend singing.

Mystabella and Rainbow Sparkles love the world they live in and care about the environment. They have a shared mission to help all the creatures of the world by cleaning up pollution and anything that destroys the environment.

Word Wizard

Rainbow Sparkles has been reading about how to help the planet! Find all the words she learned.

ANIMALS
ENVIRONMENT
CARE
RECYCLE
WILDLIFE

CLEAN UP
CONSERVATION
ECOLOGICAL
GREEN
NATURE RESERVE

AWESOME!

```
L A C I G O L O C E T C V
E E O N A D U S U N T O I
R A B C O E S G E R C N X
A L T V C B K M N D E S G
T B L A E P N H T C T E Y
A E T C F O G X L G O R K
N A T U R E R E S E R V E
L G U I M E A C A R P A F
N Y V Z C N J I B A C T E
B N B Y U A J V T C T I L
E Z C P F G R E E N C O R
S L A M I N A E K A L N K
E R U F I W I L D L I F E
```

Messy Maze

Help Rainbow Sparkles collect all the candy wrappers and put them in the recycling bin!

Joyful Jokers

Mystabella and Rainbow Sparkles are terrible at making jokes, but they love to laugh. Read on and see if a few of their favorites make you smile.

Q. Why are all unicorns so healthy?

A. Because they eat a *stable* diet.

Q. What did one raindrop say to the other?

A. Two's company, three's a *cloud*.

Q. What do you do if you see an angry star?

A. Give it some space!

Q. What do you call a sheep with no legs?

A. A cloud.

Q. What bows can't be tied?

A. Rainbows!

A unicorn goes to see the doctor and says, "Doctor, I'm worried something is wrong. I have a terribly sore throat." The doctor assures her, "It's okay, you're just a little *horse*."

Crazy Code

Mystabella and Rainbow Sparkles have been joking around. Crack the code to find the punch line!

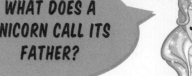

WHAT DOES A UNICORN CALL ITS FATHER?

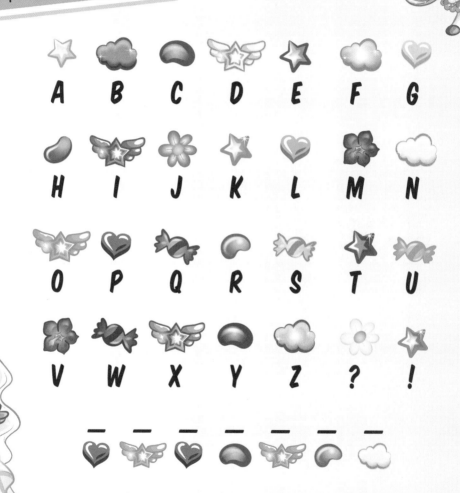

A B C D E F G

H I J K L M N

O P Q R S T U

V W X Y Z ? !

_ _ _ _ _ _ _

20

Sudoku Star

Fill in this sudoku grid with one of each item in every row and column.

Great Grid

Use the grid to trace, draw, and then color in Rainbow Sparkles!

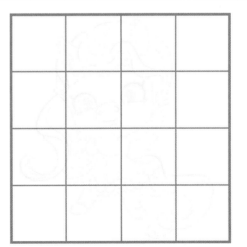

Picture Perfect

Rainbow Sparkles needs to be brightened up! Can you color in the picture above?

Answers

Page 4
Rainbow Rush
2 is the fastest route.

Page 5
Unique Unicorn
4 is the real Rainbow Sparkles.

Sugary Shadows
1 is the real shadow.

Page 16
Word Wizard

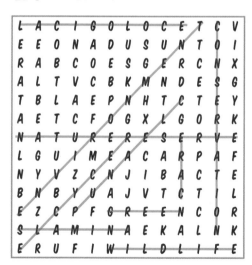

Page 17
Messy Maze

Page 20
Crazy Code
Popcorn

Page 21
Sudoku Star
A=4, B=2, C=1, D=3